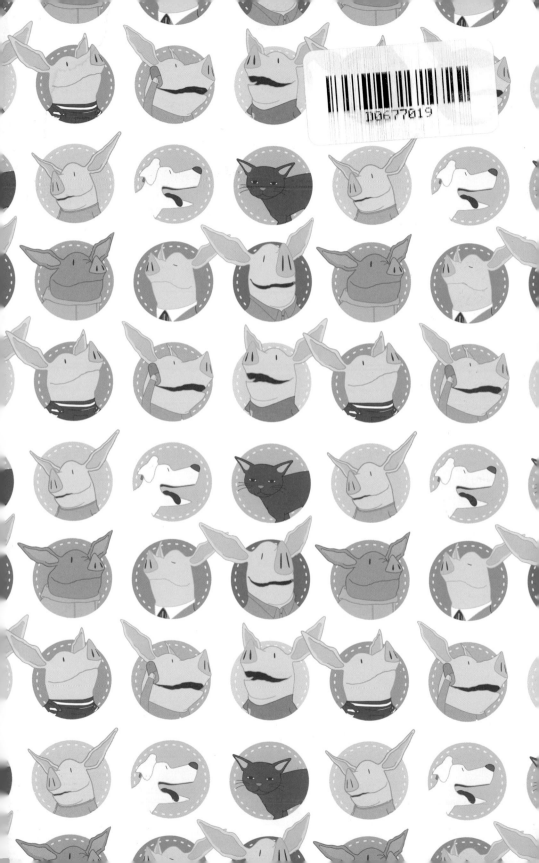

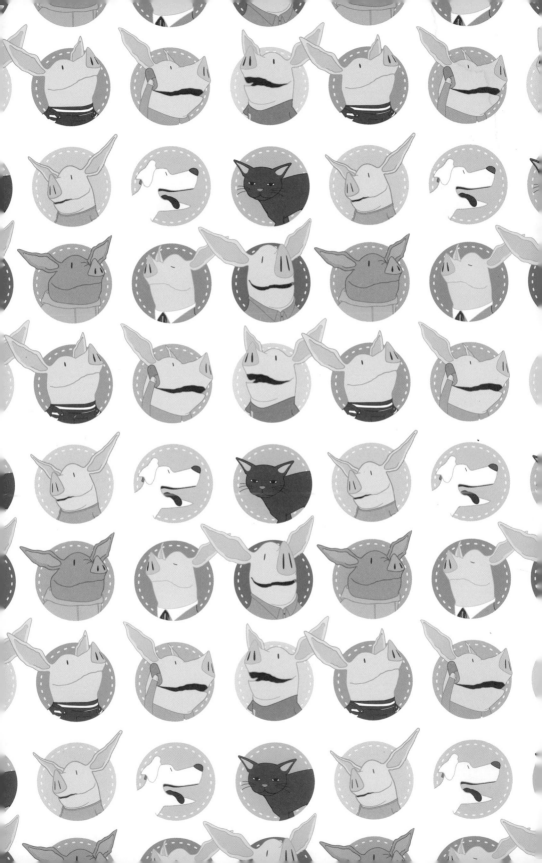

OLIVIA™

and the Kite Party

adapted by Alex Harvey
based on the screenplay "Kite Season" written by Jack Monaco
illustrated by Patrick Spaziante

Ready-to-Read

Simon Spotlight
New York   London   Toronto   Sydney   New Delhi

Whoosh!
It is a very windy day.
Olivia smiles.
It is a perfect day
to fly kites!

"Mom, do you have anything we can use to make kites?" Olivia asks.

"Well," Mom says. "We have ribbons, streamers, and bows. I do not know how you can make a kite out of them."

"Leave that to me,"
Olivia says.

After a while Ian says,
"I am done."
"Very nice," Olivia tells him.
"Are you ready to try it out?"

"But we need string,"
Ian says.
Olivia asks Francine for help.
"I have something even
better," Francine says.
"Yarn!"

"Do you want to make a kite?" Olivia asks Francine.
"There is enough wind for one hundred kites. It could be a party!"

Francine is excited.
"A kite party!" she says.

On pieces of paper,
Olivia writes:
"You are invited to our
kite party . . ."

When she is done,
she folds the papers into
paper airplanes . . .
and sends them flying out
the window!

Later, everyone gathers
with their kites.
"Great kites!" Olivia says.
"Is everybody ready?"
"Ready!" everyone says.

But Daisy has no kite.
"Where is yours, Daisy?"
asks Olivia.
"At home," Daisy says.
"There is no wind!"

Olivia looks around.
"Where did the wind go?"
she asks.
"Maybe the wind blew the
wind away," Ian says.

"I guess we will just have to
save the kites for another
day," says Mom.
"Sorry, Olivia, no wind,
no kites," Francine adds.

"Wait, so what if there is
no wind?" Olivia asks.
"We made our own kites.
Now you want us to
make it windy?" Daisy asks.

"We can all blow air!"
Ian says.
Everyone blows, but
nothing happens.
"We are not windy enough,"
says Ian.

"We just need to think bigger," Olivia says. "Much bigger." Now everyone has a paper fan. They start waving when Olivia tells them to.

"And one, and two . . ."
But it does not work.
Olivia thinks.
"There is only one thing to do.
Think WAY bigger!" she says.

A short time later,
Olivia and Ian create
a windmill using a teepee,
canoe paddles, fans,
and a bicycle!

Ian starts to pedal.

"It is working!" Olivia shouts.

"We have wind!"

"I do not think I have seen so many kites in the sky," Mom says.
"Looks like yours is ready," Dad tells Olivia.

"It just needs
one more thing,"
Olivia says.
She adds a big red O
to her kite.

"Now it is perfect!"
says Olivia.
She lets go of the kite
and it flies high in the sky!

OLIVIA™
and the Rain Dance

adapted by Maggie Testa
based on the screenplay "Olivia Makes it Rain"
written by Michael Stern
illustrated by Guy Wolek

Ready-to-Read

Simon Spotlight
New York   London   Toronto   Sydney   New Delhi

Olivia, Ian, and Francine
are going to the park.
They will have a boat race.

"Hey, where is the water?"
asks Ian.

"It has not rained in weeks," says Mr. Greengrass. "It might not rain again for a long time."

"If only I could control the weather," says Olivia.
That gives Olivia an idea.
"I wonder . . ."

"We can make it rain!"
she says.
Olivia, Francine, and Ian
dress up for a rain dance.

"Just do what I do,"
says Olivia.
"Reach to the sky!"

Now spin like a top!"

"And now just do whatever you want!" says Olivia.

Drip, drop!
"It is working!" cries Olivia.

"It is only Ian,"
says Francine.
But Ian gives Olivia an idea.

"We can fill up the pond with the hose," she says. Olivia, Ian, and Francine pull . . . and pull . . . and pull.

But the hose is not long
enough.
"Pull harder," says Olivia.

Francine drops the hose.
Olivia and Ian go flying!
"Oops, sorry!" cries
Francine.

Olivia has another idea—
water balloons!
"How will we get all these
water balloons to the pond?"
asks Francine.

Olivia smiles.
She knows just what to do.
"Ready! Aim! Fire!"
she commands.

Splat!

"We cannot have a boat race without water," says Ian.

Olivia sees Connor go by
on his skateboard.
She knows just what to do!
"We can have a
boat race without water!"

"Follow me!" says Olivia.

"Welcome to Olivia's first annual toy boat race— on dry land!" says Olivia.

Go, Ian!
Go, Francine!
Go, Olivia!

It is a three-way tie!
Then *boom*!
It starts to thunder.
Then it starts to rain.

It is still raining
at bedtime.
Olivia smiles.
They can have a
water boat race tomorrow.

OLIVIA™
Goes Camping

adapted by Alex Harvey
based on the screenplay written by Patrick Resnick
illustrated by Jared Osterhold

Ready-to-Read

Simon Spotlight
New York   London   Toronto   Sydney

Olivia and her family
are going camping.

Olivia's best friend,
Francine, is going too.

Francine does not think
she likes camping.
"I will get dirty and wet,"
she says.

"Camping is fun," Olivia tells her.

"There are five things you must do on a great camping trip."

"Number one: watch my dad try to put up the tent."

"He will forget to put in all the poles.

And the tent will fall

down!"

"Dad always needs my help," Olivia says.

Olivia tells Francine to use
the hammer to bang the
tent stake into the ground.

"Now, the number two thing is to climb a mountain."

"But my foot hurts,"
Francine says.

"Do you want to lie down?"
Olivia asks.
"I will get dirty if I lie
down," says Francine.
Olivia says that getting
dirty is part of camping.

It is number three on her
list.
"But I don't want to get
dirty," Francine says.

Francine brought her blanket, pillow, and cot. Olivia brought her sleeping bag.

Number four on Olivia's list: find a really cool bug.

"Ow! I got bitten by a mosquito," Francine says.

"That doesn't count," says
Olivia.

"But it itches," Francine says.

"Mud is great for bug bites,"
Olivia says.

"Eww! I am dirty and wet
and covered with mud!"
Francine cries.
"I need a shower!"

Olivia ties a bag of water
to a tree branch.
Then she pokes holes
in the bag.

Water spills out . . .
like a shower!

"Cool!" says Francine.

Olivia tells Francine that
number five on the list
is to find a perfect stick
to roast marshmallows.

"One end of the stick
must be sharp," says Olivia.
"But not too sharp!"

"This stick has too many branches.

This one is too long . . .

and this one is too short."

"How about this one?"

Francine asks.

"Perfect!" says Olivia.
"You are a great camper,
Francine."

OLIVIA™
Plants a Garden

adapted by Emily Sollinger
based on the screenplay written by Rachel Ruderman
and Laurie Israel
illustrated by Jared Osterhold

Ready-to-Read

Simon Spotlight
New York   London   Toronto   Sydney

"It is springtime, children!"
says Mrs. Hoggenmuller.
"We will plant our own gardens.

"Each student will get
a packet of seeds.
You will plant
the seeds at home."

"What will we grow?"
asks Olivia.

"Sprouts, herbs, flowers,
and beans,"
says Mrs. Hoggenmuller.
"Come choose your seeds!"

"What kind of seeds
are these?" asks Olivia.
"I do not know,"
says Mrs. Hoggenmuller.

"These are surprise seeds."

At home Olivia digs in
her yard.
Perry helps her dig.

"This is going to be the best surprise garden ever," she tells Julian.

"Did you know that talking to plants can help them grow faster?" asks Father.

"I can do that!" says Olivia.

"Hello, plants," says Olivia.
"I hope that you grow
so I will know what you are."

Olivia tells her plants
lots of stories.
She shows her plants
how she rides a scooter.
She sings songs to her
plants.

Oh no!

Perry is digging a hole

right where Olivia planted

her seeds.

"Oh, Perry!" says Olivia.
"I will just have to
plant more seeds.
And I will have to be even
more patient."

"Look!" says Olivia.
She holds up a bone.
"I think it is a
dinosaur bone."

"I am not sure," says Julian.

"I found a dinosaur bone
in my garden,"
says Olivia at school.
"I do not think that is

a dinosaur bone,"
says Mrs. Hoggenmuller.
"I think it is a dog toy.
Look! It is attracting flies."

Back at her house,
Olivia checks on her plants.
"My surprise seeds have
grown into surprise plants!"

All of the children bring
their plants to school.
"This is my surprise plant!"
says Olivia.
Snap!
Olivia's plant closes around
a fly.

"That is a Venus flytrap,"
says Mrs. Hoggenmuller.
"I will call it a surprise plant,"
says Olivia.
"That fly sure looked
surprised!"

"You did a wonderful job with your garden," says Father at bedtime. "I do not think we will have any more flies," says Olivia. "Good night, Olivia!"

OLIVIA™
Takes a Trip

adapted by Ellie O'Ryan
based on the screenplay "OLIVIA Takes a Road Trip"
written by Eric Shaw
illustrated by Jared Osterhold

Ready-to-Read

Simon Spotlight
New York   London   Toronto   Sydney

Olivia and her family
are taking a trip.
Olivia is excited to fly
on a plane!

Olivia packs her trunk.
She packs clothes and
her favorite toy.

Ian packs a small
lunch box.
"This is my suitcase!"
Ian says.

Dad has some bad news.

A big storm is coming.

The plane cannot fly

in the storm.

They will drive the car
to Grandma's house
instead.
Olivia is sad.
She wanted to fly
on a plane!

Julian comes over

to say good-bye.

He has a present for Olivia.

It is a walkie-talkie!

Olivia and her family
get in the car.

"Are we there yet?" Ian asks.

The walkie-talkie is lou

It wakes up William!

William starts to cry.

Olivia wishes she were
on a plane.

The car ride is boring.

At the gas station Olivia
helps Dad wash the
windshield.

Dad's brush has soap on it.
Olivia's brush is muddy.
Dad has to wash the
windshield again!

Mom buys an ice pop for
Olivia and Ian to share.
Olivia wants the red part.
Ian wants the red part too!

The ice pop lands on the car.
Dad has to wash the
windshield again.
"We will never get
to Grandma's house!"
Olivia says.

Olivia has an idea.

She will imagine that

she is on a plane!

"Welcome to Air Olivia!"
Captain Olivia says.

Olivia's plane has a movie
for Dad to watch.
And popcorn for Dad to eat.
There is a yummy dinner
for Mom.

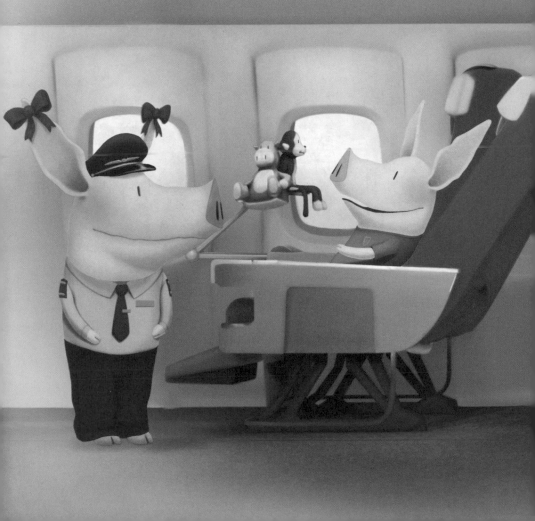

And a red rose for Mom, too.
"This is the best plane ever!"
Mom says.

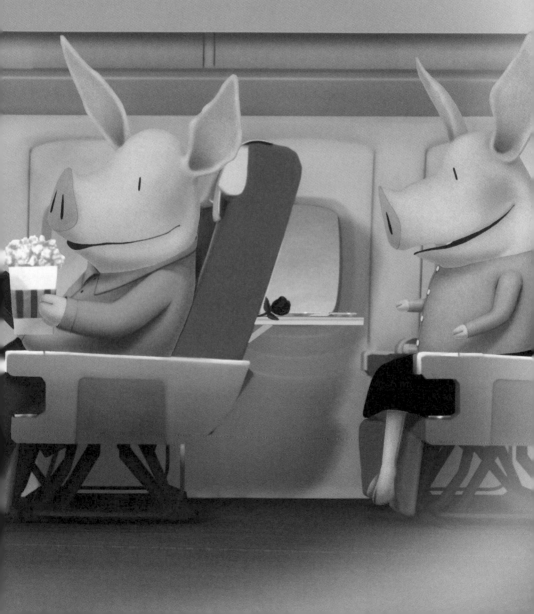

Captain Olivia tells her family to put on their seat belts.

Captain Olivia sees dark clouds out the window.

"Uh-oh!" says Olivia.
"Dark clouds mean
a storm is coming."

"We will fly around the storm," Captain Olivia says. The plane loops around a rainbow.

It flies past the storm!

"We are at Grandma's
house!" Olivia shouts.
She gives Grandma
a big hug.

OLIVIA™
Builds a House

adapted by Maggie Testa
based on the screenplay "Little Big House" written by Jule Selbo
illustrated by Shane L. Johnson

Ready-to-Read

Simon Spotlight
New York   London   Toronto   Sydney   New Delhi

This is Olivia.
And this is her father.
Father builds houses.
That is his job.

Before Father builds a house,
he makes a model of it.

Olivia likes to help
build the model houses.

Father has a new client, Mrs. Hickory. She wants to see this model house.

But first Father
has to pick her up
from the airport.
Olivia will keep
the model safe
while he is gone.

Olivia is happy to help!

Edwin, no!

Perry, no!

Olivia needs to find
a safer spot
for the model house.

"No one can come
into the living room!"
says Olivia.
"I must keep the model
house safe."

"Perry, no!" cries Ian.
But it is too late.

"This is not good,"
says Olivia.

"What can we do?" asks Ian.

Olivia knows what to do!
They can put the model
together again.

"All done!" says Olivia.
But something is not right.
"This does not look like a
house," says Ian.

Olivia knows what to do!
They will build a new
model house.

This one will be bigger
and fancier and redder.

"It just needs one more thing!" says Olivia.

"There," she says.
"It is perfectly perfect."
"Just in time," says Ian.
"Father is home!"

Mrs. Hickory looks at
the model house.
"How did you know that red
is my favorite color?"
she asks Olivia.

"Simple," replies Olivia.
"It is everyone's favorite
color."
Mrs. Hickory turns to Father.
"You are hired!" she says.

Later, Father tucks Olivia
into bed.
"Your model was amazing!
Thank you for all your help.
Good night, Olivia!"

OLIVIA™
Trains Her Cat

adapted by Sarah Albee, based on the screenplay
"Olivia and Her Trained Cat" written by Joe Purdy
illustrated by Shane L. Johnson

Ready-to-Read

Simon Spotlight
New York   London   Toronto   Sydney

"My cat, Gwendolyn, can
jump," says Francine.
"Wow!" all of the kids say.
"And Gwendolyn can also
walk on her back legs,"
says Francine.

"My cat, Edwin, can dance ballet!" says Olivia.

"Wow!" all of the kids say.

"Gwendolyn can cook,"
says Francine.
"So can Edwin!"
says Olivia.

"Your cats sound special," says Mrs. Hoggenmuller. "Can you bring your cats for show-and-tell?"

"We can have a pet talent contest!" says Olivia.

"Great idea!"

says Mrs. Hoggenmuller.

"Edwin just likes to sleep,"
says Julian.
"Will Edwin do tricks?"
Olivia is sure that
Edwin will.

"Okay, Edwin, jump!"
commands Olivia.
Edwin keeps sleeping.

"If you jump through
this hoop, you can
have a fish!"
Edwin just snores.

"Is something wrong, Olivia?" asks Mother.

"Edwin will not do tricks!" says Olivia sadly.

"He just sleeps!"

"It is hard to get an old cat to do tricks," says Mother.

"But Francine has a cat that will do tricks!" groans Olivia.

The next day at school,
the talent show begins.
"My hamster can eat
a carrot," says Daisy.
Everyone claps.

"My parrot can say 'hi,'"
says Harold.

"Hi, there!" says the parrot.

Everyone claps.

"This is my lizard,"
says Julian.
"He can catch a fly."
Everyone claps.

"This is my cat, Edwin,"
says Olivia.

"Edwin can do many tricks."

"Jump, Edwin!" says Olivia.
Edwin sleeps.

Oh, no! Olivia worries.

"Okay, then, sleep, Edwin!"
Edwin sleeps.
"Snore, Edwin!"
Edwin snores.
Everyone claps.

Francine goes next.

"Meet Gwendolyn."

She can walk on

her back legs.

She can flip backward.

She can jump
through a hoop.

"I think we have a winner!
The winner is Gwendolyn!"
says Mrs. Hoggenmuller.

After school Olivia
and Julian go to her house.
"Edwin should have won,"
says Julian.

Olivia looks around.
"Where is Edwin?"
Olivia and Julian
search and search.

Olivia and Julian go
to Francine's house.
They find Gwendolyn.
They also find Edwin
doing tricks!

OLIVIA™
Measures Up

adapted by Maggie Testa
based on the screenplay written by Patricia Resnick
illustrated by Jared Osterhold

Ready-to-Read

Simon Spotlight
New York   London   Toronto   Sydney   New Delhi

It is a big day for Olivia!
She is finally tall enough
to go on the big-kid rides
at the amusement park!

Ian wants to go
on the big-kid rides too.

But he is not tall enough.

Whee!
Olivia loves the
roller coaster.

After the ride, Father tells
Olivia that Ian will probably
be bigger than her
when they grow up.

Olivia does not like
the sound of that!

At lunchtime Ian wants to drink some milk.
"That is a good choice," says Father.
"Milk will make you tall."

Olivia offers Ian
a glass of water.
"Milk," says Ian.
"How about lemonade?"
Olivia asks.
"Milk," Ian repeats.

Back at home,
Olivia drinks some milk
and calls Julian.

If Ian will not stop growing,
then Olivia will just
grow faster.
"Pull harder," says Olivia.

"If you keep growing,
you will not be able to
ride your bike,"
Olivia tells Ian.

"Or play hide-and-seek,"
adds Julian.
"That sounds terrible,"
says Ian.
"I will try to stop growing."

"How tall will I be when I grow up?" Ian asks Father. "You will be about my height," replies Father.

"Can you ride a bike?
Can you play hide-and-seek?"
Ian asks Father.
Father answers yes and yes.

Ian decides that he will grow. "You are making a big mistake," says Olivia.

"Little brothers
should not be taller than
their big sisters!"

The next day is
picture day at school.

Olivia wants to stand
in the back row, but she
is not tall enough.

But that does not stop Olivia!

Smile, everyone!

Before bed Father explains
something to Olivia.
"Even if Ian grows taller,
you will always be
his big sister."